DISCARD

Principal Fred
Won't GO TO Bed

by

Carolyn Crimi

illustrated by

Donald Wu

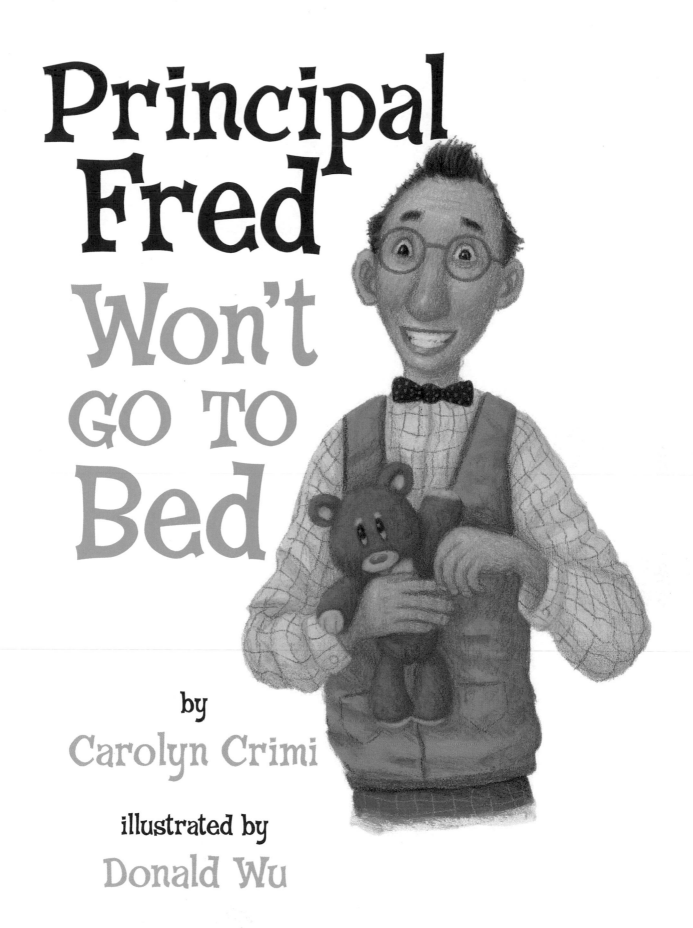

two lions

two lions

Text copyright © 2010 by Carolyn Crimi
Illustrations copyright © 2010 by Donald Wu
All rights reserved
Amazon Publishing, Attn: Amazon Children's Publishing, P.O. Box 400818,
Las Vegas, NV 89140
www.amazon.com/amazonchildrenspublishing

Library of Congress Cataloging-in-Publication Data

Crimi, Carolyn.
Principal Fred won't go to bed / by Carolyn Crimi ; illustrated by Donald
Wu. — 1st ed.
p. cm.
Summary: At bedtime, Principal Fred's wife, son, and dog help him search
for his missing teddy bear so that he can go to sleep.
ISBN 978-1-4778-1602-8
[1. Stories in rhyme. 2. Lost and found possessions—Fiction. 3.
Bedtime—Fiction. 4. Teddy bears—Fiction. 5. School principals—Fiction. 6.
Humorous stories.] I. Wu, Donald, ill. II. Title. III. Title: Principal
Fred will not go to bed.
PZ8.3.C8715Pri 2010
[E]—dc22
2009028848

The illustrations are rendered in mixed medium, acrylic and color pencils.
Book design by Anahid Hamparian
Editor: Margery Cuyler

*For the students, teachers, and principals
who have welcomed me into their schools,
and for Carol, who makes it all happen*
—C.C.

For Barron
—D.W.

The school day was over
for Principal Fred.

After his dinner,
he went up to bed.

He slipped into jammies,
but it wasn't too long
before he discovered
that something was WRONG.

"WHERE IS MY BEAR?"
yelled Principal Fred.
"I can't sleep without him!
I won't go to bed!"

His wife brought his blankie—
Fred looked near a chair.
Young Ned brought his slippers—
his fuzziest pair.

They brought him a tray
with warm cookies and milk.
Big Jake dragged his robe
made of checkereds blue silk.

They searched every nook!
They looked everywhere!
But no one could find
that scrappy, old bear.

"I need Bear!" Fred yelled,
as he raced down the stairs.

He zigged and he zagged
and he hopped across chairs.

His family was panicked.
Where could Bear be?

Under a table?

Under a tree?

They dashed and they crashed
into bathrooms and halls.
They shouted and barked
as they bumped into walls.

Fred ran to the kitchen—
zip-zippity zoom!
Then he slipped on a sock—

bang-bangity-BOOM!

"OUCH! Oooh, that hurts!
There's a bump on my head!
I need my bear NOW,
or I won't go to bed!"

But just then Big Jake
let out a small *yip!*
He nudged that old sock
and gave it a nip.

"THERE'S MY POOR BEAR!
You found him, Big Jake!
You deserve a fresh bone,
or better yet, steak!"

They clapped and they cheered,
"Hip hip hooray!"
They danced 'round in circles;
Big Jake saved the day!

Big Jake ate his treat
as he lay on the floor.
Fred tiptoed upstairs
when Jake started to snore.

"Good night," Fred said, yawning, and climbed into bed.

His wife whispered softly,
"Sweet dreams, sleepyhead."

The following day
was breezy and bright,
but Principal Fred
woke up with a fright.

"WHERE IS MY BEAR?"

yelled Principal Fred.
"I won't leave without him!
I'm staying in bed!"

Carolyn Crimi

has written a number of popular children's books, including *The Louds Move In!*, *Henry and the Buccaneer Bunnies*, and *Boris and Bella*. She lives in Evanston, Illinois, with her husband and her pug, who sometimes goes by the name of Sir Scratch and Sniff. To learn more about the author, visit: www.carolyncrimi.com

Donald Wu

was born in Hong Kong but grew up in the San Francisco Bay area, where he spent many days doodling in school. Currently, his favorite medium is colored pencils over acrylic, although he also paints with watercolors. His most recent books include *Change-up: Baseball Poems* by Gene Fehler and *Dogerella* by Maribeth Boelts. Mr. Wu continues to live and doodle in the San Francisco Bay area. To learn more about the illustrator, visit: www.donald-wu.com

Made in the USA
Charleston, SC
05 April 2014